This Little Tiger book belongs to:

To Olivia
Good Luck in Year 2.
I've enjoyed working
with you this year!
with love
Mrs Taylor x (2005)

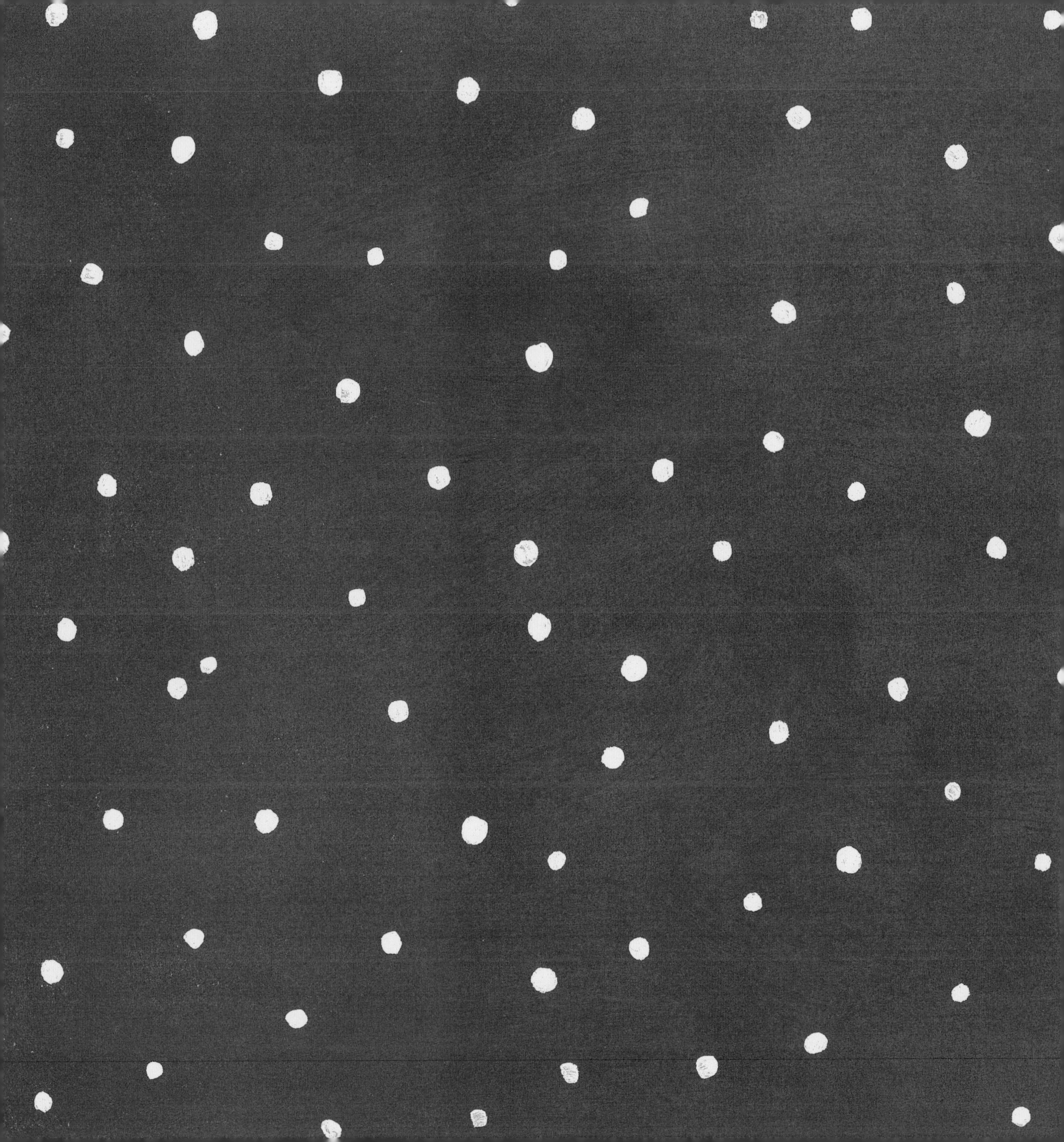

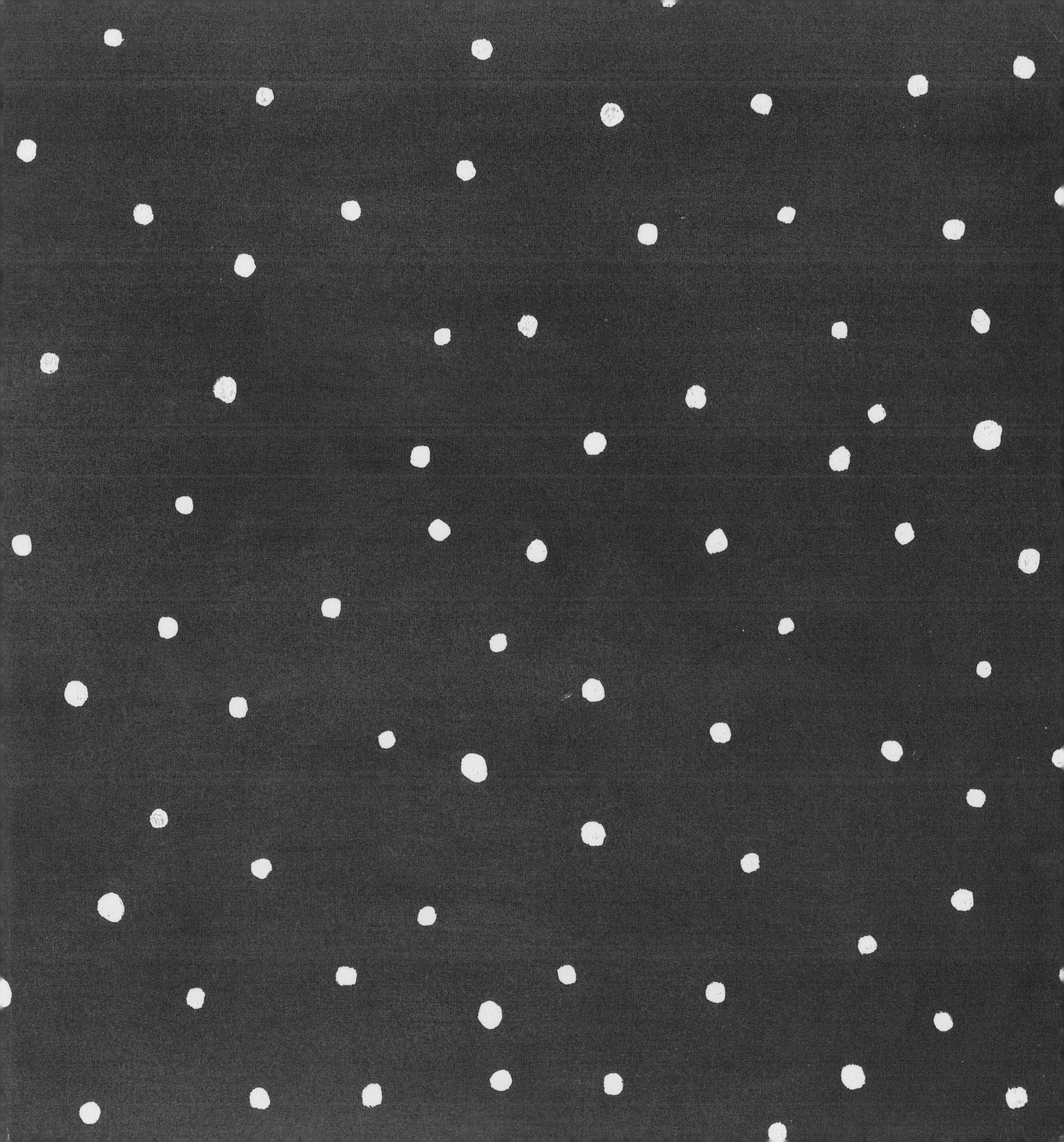

For Georgie
and Olivia

LITTLE TIGER PRESS
An imprint of Magi Publications
1 The Coda Centre, 189 Munster Road,
London SW6 6AW
www.littletigerpress.com
First published in Great Britain 2003
This paperback edition published 2004

Printed in Malaysia •
ISBN 1 85430 872 6
1 3 5 7 9 10 8 6 4 2

Tim Warnes

Happy Birthday, Dotty!

LITTLE TIGER PRESS
London

Dotty was very excited.
It was her birthday, and she
had lots of cards to open.

But where were all Dotty's friends?

Dotty went to find Pip the mouse. Instead she found a little round present with her name on it!

What could it be?

Hooray!

A bouncy ball!

As she chased after it, Dotty spotted an arrow on the floor. It pointed to another and another.

It was a birthday trail! Dotty followed the arrows . . .

. . . to the sandpit, where there was *another* parcel. Dotty read the label. "Happy Birthday, Dotty, love from Tommy the tortoise."

What was it?

Delicious!

A yummy bone!

Dotty hurried across
the garden, following
the arrows to . . .

. . . Susie's apple tree.
Leaning against
her nest was
another present!

Yippee!

It was a kite from Susie!

But Susie wasn't there to help fly it.
Where was everyone?

Dotty was puzzled.
Taking all her presents,
she skipped along the trail
of arrows to . . .

. . .Whiskers the rabbit's hutch.
Dotty saw another funny-shaped present.
She read, "Happy Birthday, Dotty,
love from Whiskers."

Dotty began to
unwrap it . . .

Wow!

A trike!

Dotty squealed with delight. She popped all her presents into the trailer. She'd had lots of surprises, but still Dotty's friends were nowhere to be seen.

Where could they be? Maybe they had followed the arrows too. Dotty climbed on to her shiny new trike and . . .

WHEEE!

She went to look for her friends.

Suddenly the trail ended.
Dotty was amazed to find . . .

. . . the

BIGGEST PRESENT

she had ever seen!

Dotty danced round
and round in circles.
What could this be?

"SURPRISE!
HAPPY BIRTHDAY,
DOTTY!"